Freckle Stars

To Mary,
Keep reading
and reach for the
Stars! Thanks
for having me on
The Rhode Show!
8 March 2017

JACKIE LEDUC

PAGE PUBLISHING, INC.
New York, NY

First originally published by Page Publishing, Inc. 2017

ISBN 978-1-68409-131-7 (Paperback)
ISBN 978-1-68409-132-4 (Digital)

Printed in the United States of America

Freckle Stars

There once was a girl named Clementine who hated her freckles.

At school, the children poked fun at her. They called her names. Her friends even tried to connect the dots with a pen. This made Clementine really annoyed.

Clementine wanted to get rid of her freckles. The only people that had liked them were her mother and the bus driver. He complimented them the first day of school, but that made no difference. She hated her freckles and wanted them gone.

Clementine thought long and hard.

Then she got an idea.

"Chalk is white. If I spread enough of that on me, I'll look normal."

So then, Clementine spread chalk all over her arms, legs, and face. Only problem was, it was itchy. Soon, red patches appeared on her skin. She had no choice but to wash it off.

One day, seeing her mother putting makeup on in the mirror, Clementine came up with another idea. When her mother left, Clementine spread this tan makeup her mother had called foundation on her skin. Her freckles were completely gone!

Clementine went to school happy that they were gone. She was sure everyone would like her now. She went into class, but instead of compliments, everyone laughed. The morning rain had washed the makeup off, leaving streaks everywhere on her skin. Clementine looked a mess!

She ran to the bathroom. Wiping off the makeup, she began to cry.

"Why do I have to have such ugly spots? Why can't I just be normal?"

When she got home, Clementine told her mother the story.

To this, her mother then said, "Do you know what freckles are? They are stars. You see, when you are awake, they become part of your skin. When you are asleep, the stars go into the sky."

Clementine then asked her mother, "Well then, how is it that when I am awake, I can see stars in the sky?"

"Because, darling, there are other children with freckles just like you. When you see stars, they are asleep."

21

Clementine thought it over and was amazed.

"I have stars on my skin. That is the coolest thing ever."

She finally realized that freckles were the best and that other people were just jealous. Clementine was glad about the way she was, at last.

About the Author

Photograph by Doreen Roy

Jackie Leduc is the author of two highly rated novels *The Demonic Eyes* and *Bloody Nightmares*. She decided to write *Freckle Stars* to empower other children with freckles to embrace their unique beauty. Leduc lives in Massachusetts where she currently attends high school. She spends her time—when not writing—taking photographs, volunteering in her community, and reading lots of books. If you would like to know more about Leduc, her other books and events, you can find her at

Twitter, @authorjleduc
Facebook page, Jackie Leduc
Instagram, @the_demonic_eyes

CPSIA information can be obtained
at www.ICGtesting.com
Printed in the USA
BVOW05s0820260217
477058BV00004B/3/P